MR PERFECT

TIM COLLINS

Mr Perfect ISBN 978-1-78464-325-6

Publisher: Susan Ross
Senior Editor: Danny Pearson
Editorial Coordinator: Claire Morgan
Copyeditor: Cheryl Lanyon
Designer: Bigtop Design Ltd
Printed by Bell and Bain Ltd, Glasgow

2 4 6 8 10 9 7 5 3 1

CHAPTER 1

Have you ever met someone totally perfect for you? I did and it was horrible.

A few weeks ago, Dad told me he was going to a robotics convention in New York. It fell over the half-term break, so I assumed he'd take me along for a week of shopping and sightseeing. I assumed wrong. He said I had to stay with my uncle Simon in a tiny village called Snarehill instead.

This was an uncle I hadn't even seen in a decade, so it wasn't like I'd be catching up with a beloved relative or anything. I'd be waiting around in the middle of nowhere with some old guy I didn't even know.

At least it would get me away from my personal robot, Sarah. She's a really old model. Over five years old, in fact. I can't even install any new personality updates on her because she's so out-of-date.

You'd think having a robotics engineer for a dad would mean you'd always have the newest and best robots. Not if you're me.

Dad had always refused to work for a big robotics firm because he was developing his own secret project in our basement. In the meantime, I had to get by with a robot about as advanced as a pocket calculator.

Sarah shuffled into my room as I was packing my suitcase the night before I had to leave.

"Let me help you with your task," said Sarah. She headed over to my wardrobe, but froze along the way. Her clear, flat voice switched into a fast mumble. "I need a cab to get me to the airport for half seven."

Sarah had developed a fault that meant she'd broadcast other people's phone calls in the

MR PERFECT

Titles in Teen Reads:

Badger Publishing Limited, Oldmedow Road, Hardwick Industrial Estate, King's Lynn PE30 4JJ
Telephone: 01438 791037

www.badgerlearning.co.uk

middle of our conversations. One minute I'd be chatting with her about school, and the next I'd hear Mr Flanagan from number 43 talking to his mistress in a gross sexy voice.

But if Sarah had been working properly, I'd never have found out the real reason I was being sent to my uncle's house.

"Seven whole days in the middle of nowhere," I said to Sarah as I threw a pair of jeans into the open case on my bed. "This is going to be awful."

"It must be very upsetting for you," said Sarah.

Sarah's stilted voice cut out and I heard my father instead.

"Until next Saturday," he was saying. "I've told her I'm going to a conference in New York… She'll arrive at the house tomorrow afternoon… It's a Turing test for my M35–50… I've got really high hopes for it…"

Dad's phone call cut out and Sarah's voice cut in again. "I have a lot of sympathy for you…"

"Shh!" I said.

So Dad wasn't sending me away for a break at all. He was tricking me into taking part in a Turing test – a test to see if a robot can pass for a human.

No doubt my uncle would introduce me to some mysterious villager who would turn out to be a robot and Dad would call himself a genius because I failed to catch on.

I was about to rush downstairs and have a go at him when I had a better idea. I'd go along to the village, meet his robot and totally fail to be convinced by it.

It would upset him, but he deserved it for forcing me to take part in his mean experiment. He'd only have himself to blame.

CHAPTER 2

I arrived at Snarehill station just after noon on the following Sunday. The server robots get older and slower as you travel out of the city. It's amazing how behind the times everything is.

The robot that drove me from the station to my uncle's house was really old, with an external battery pack and fingers that didn't bend at the knuckles. He even ran through a couple of red lights, which meant his eye circuits must have been on the way out. When we arrived, I tipped him ten credits and told him to treat himself to an upgrade.

My uncle welcomed me inside and we had an awkward conversation. He works from home, doing some dull financial job or other. After an especially long pause I told him I needed some fresh air and went off to search for the robot.

My uncle's next-door neighbour was an overweight, middle-aged man with grey hair, called Malcolm. If this was Dad's new model, I didn't think much of the design. I couldn't imagine many robot fans camping out all night to be the first to own him.

There was a woman in the village shop called Magda. It took her ages to find her glasses and operate the till when I tried to buy a chocolate bar. She didn't exactly scream 'brand new' either.

It wasn't until the following morning that I saw him. A tall boy of about my age, with broad shoulders, wearing blue jeans and a white T-shirt. I spotted him through the kitchen window while I was eating breakfast.

I asked who the boy was. I had to snap my fingers in front of my uncle's face to draw his attention away from his tablet computer.

"Him?" said my uncle. "A boy from one of the local villages. Called Leon, I think. He offered his services as a gardener while he's on half term and didn't ask for much."

"So he's only here for this week?" I asked. "What a coincidence!"

I thought Dad could have made up a more convincing excuse for the robot to be there. After all that time building it, he could have worked a little harder on his cover story.

I knew my uncle would be reporting back to Dad, so I decided to get their hopes up by talking to the robot. The more it looked like I was falling for their scheme, the more disappointed they'd be in the end.

Leon was raking leaves into a black plastic bag. I gazed at him as I approached. Dad had done an amazing job. His dark hair was cropped short and looked nothing like the fake stuff you usually see on robots. I could even see tiny black dots on his chin and under his nose as though he'd recently shaved. The attention to detail was brilliant.

When he looked up at me, I was astonished by how lifelike his eyes were. They were light blue, and his pupils shrank as he turned to the light, just as real eyes would.

He stared at me and I found myself looking away, like I would if a real boy tried to hold my gaze. This was pathetic. I couldn't make eye contact with a robot.

"I'm Rachel," I said. "I'm staying here for the next few days. School holidays."

I wondered how long Dad had been working on Leon. He could have sold the eyes alone to a big robotics firm for billions of credits. It was typical of him to insist on working alone instead of making us rich.

"I'm Leon," he said, wiping the soil from

his hands.

I swept my hair behind my ear and felt suddenly aware of my crumpled jeans and sweaty T-shirt. Did I even have any decent clothes with me?

I couldn't believe the way my thoughts were running. It's one thing to feel awkward around boys, but feeling awkward around boys who aren't even real is just silly.

I could hardly blame myself, though. Dad had designed this robot to be very attractive. Robots are often quite cute, but most of them stop short of outright hotness.

It wasn't something I'd ever expected to think, but Dad had really good taste in guys.

I tried to forget my discomfort by testing Leon's programming. I thought back to my robotics class at school. How were you meant to catch them out?

I remembered my teacher Mr Bradbury talking

about smell. Robots don't have a sense of smell, and can only repeat stock responses if you ask them about it.

"There's a really strong smell in the air," I said. "Do you know what it is?"

"It could be me," said Leon. He had a deep voice with a hint of the local accent. It was nothing like the flat monotone you usually hear from older robots. "I've been working for a few hours already."

I leaned forwards and sniffed him, something I would never have done to a real boy.

"It's not you," I said. "Don't worry."

He pointed to a green bottle of weed killer on the grass. "Could be that, I suppose. I can move it if it's bothering you."

That might have been a prepared answer. I had to push him further.

"I don't think it's that," I said. "I've been able to smell it ever since I arrived in this village."

"In that case, it must be boredom," he said, grinning. "This whole place reeks of it."

Even if Dad hadn't managed to give him a sense of smell, he'd given him a sense of humour. Impressive.

I spent most of that evening thinking about Leon. Not about how hot he was, because that would have been a really strange way to think about a robot. But let's just say I was admiring the work Dad had put in. I couldn't believe Dad had been secretly working on such a lifelike robot in the basement of our house. It had been two floors below me for the past year. It made me wish I'd been nosy enough to steal his keys and sneak into his basement.

I had to admit I'd have been totally taken in by Leon if I hadn't known he was a robot. And maybe, just maybe, I would have asked him on a date, and felt totally humiliated when I found out he was fake.

Thinking about this made me angry, and focused my mind on my original plan. As soon as I got home, I'd tell Dad that Leon was the most obvious robot I'd ever seen.

It was going to be a fitting revenge.

CHAPTER 3

I saw Leon again the next afternoon. I was sitting on a bench at the back of the house and reading a book I'd bought for the train called *New Dawn*.

"I've read that," he said, pointing at the cover. "One of my favourites."

I wished I could meet a real boy who liked reading. All the ones at my school preferred watching robot cage-fights.

"Read any other good ones recently?" I asked.

"Quite a few," he said. *"By My Side, Noticed, Raven, Remember Rosie."*

They were all books I'd read and enjoyed in the previous few months.

That's when I understood what Dad had been up to. He'd programmed Leon using details about me. For the last few months, he'd been asking me more about my tastes in things like books and music. I thought he was taking a genuine interest. Turns out it was just research.

"What sort of music are you into?" I asked.

"The Locals, The Hunted, Insectoids," he said. "That sort of thing."

He'd listed my three favourite bands. This confirmed my suspicions.

"What about you?" he asked.

"Exactly the same," I said. "It's quite a coincidence, isn't it?"

I wondered if I'd be able to detect a flash of guilt in his eyes, but he just shrugged and said, "I guess so."

It made sense. If you're going to put a robot through a Turing test, it can't know it's a robot. It must be totally convinced it's human and that its memories and opinions and experiences are real.

I began to feel sorry for Leon. He had a jumble of thoughts running through his mind, just like I did. But his were the result of the computer coding rather than an actual brain.

Leon sat down next to me on the bench and I found myself chatting to him without any of the usual awkwardness I get when I talk to boys. I wished I could meet a real boy I clicked with like that.

Then I embarrassed myself by wondering if I should just start dating Leon anyway. Everyone from school would see me with this hot guy and they'd wonder where we'd met and…

And a thousand Leons would turn up in the shops a few months later and I'd get teased for the rest of my life.

No. Just no.

The sun sank behind the oak tree at the bottom of the garden and Leon said he had to return to work.

As he was getting up, he said, "If you want to continue this chat, we could go out to The Green Man tonight. It's about a mile towards Burnham from here. I could be there at eight if you like."

I wanted to accept, but that would have been pathetic.

"No," I said, "I'd better get on with my book."

Leon's shoulders slumped. I felt a pang of sympathy, which was just insane. He was silicon and metal. He could no more feel disappointment than a toaster could feel jealous or a tumble dryer could feel happy.

So why did I feel the urge to leap up, throw my arms around him and apologise?

CHAPTER 4

I questioned my uncle at breakfast the next day. I knew Dad was a shameless liar, but I doubted my uncle was as good at being dishonest.

I didn't remember much about my uncle from when I was young, and meeting him again triggered no memories. He was slightly taller than Dad, with short black hair and small brown eyes. He was the sort of dull, middle-aged man who got on with his work without being noticed by anyone, and he had none of Dad's humour or slyness.

"Has Leon done your garden before?" I asked.

"This is the first time," he said, taking a sip of fresh orange. "He called round last week and asked if he could work on it. I like to do what I can for the local community."

"That all sounds very convenient," I said.

"Yes, I suppose it is," he said. He prodded his tablet and it made a fake typing noise.

My uncle's helper robot carried a rack of toast over with awkward, jerky movements. She was worse than Sarah. My uncle obviously had the same attitude as Dad to spending money on decent home robots.

"I hope the toast is to your satisfaction," droned the robot.

"Where exactly is Leon from?" I asked.

"I'm not sure," he said, keeping his eyes fixed on the piece of toast he was buttering. "One of the other towns around here, I think. I like to do what I can for the local community."

He seemed uncomfortable and I was glad. He

obviously hadn't expected to be questioned about his lie.

"What do his parents do?" I asked.

"You should ask him all this yourself," he said, standing up and wiping crumbs from his tablet. "I noticed you were getting on well with him yesterday."

"I bet you did," I muttered.

I went outside and found Leon pulling up dandelions at the far end of the garden. At least my uncle wouldn't be able to spy on us back there.

He looked up, gave me a brief smile and returned to his weeding. I wondered if his programming had reminded him of my rejection the day before.

"Let me help," I said.

I got down on my knees and grabbed one of the

flowers at the bottom of its stem. I tried to yank it but it was stuck fast.

Leon put his hand around mine and helped me drag the roots out of the soil.

I'm not a flirty type. I'm really, really not. I'm the opposite, in fact. But I let Leon guide my hand around the flowerbed as we pulled up more of the weeds. I thought of it as good practice for all the real flirting with real boys I'd do one day.

After a few minutes I got up and fetched us glasses of iced orange from the kitchen. I sipped mine and watched him glug his, half expecting sparks to fly out of his mouth.

I wondered how much work Dad had put into the robot's memories, so I asked him what he could recall about his early childhood.

It turned out Dad had put a lot of work in. Leon had vague memories about being a toddler and going to school for the first time, just as a real human would.

I remembered Mr Bradbury saying that even very sophisticated robots would give themselves away by repeating themselves, so I kept pressing him on the details.

Leon passed this test too. He said a lot of things that were similar, but never exactly the same.

At one point he mentioned a childhood trip to the seaside. He'd been really excited on the way there, looking forward to making sandcastles and paddling in the sea.

But rainclouds had gathered as they drove and it was tipping down by the time they arrived. His parents had stayed in the car, but he'd been allowed to go out with an umbrella and look at the rock pools. He spent all afternoon popping seaweed and watching crabs scuttle between rocks. He soon realised he was having more fun on the cold, windy beach than he ever would have done in the sunshine.

I felt my cheeks flushing. That wasn't his memory. It was mine.

Anger welled up inside me. So Dad hadn't just stolen my tastes to program Leon. He'd stolen my memories.

The rainy seaside trip was a precious memory for me. I thought it might be precious for Dad too, but he'd obviously just seen it as raw material for his programming.

I wondered what other events from my past Dad had used in his robot. Were all my childhood tantrums, birthday parties and Christmas presents going to be implanted in every M35–50?

What about Mum? Would the story of her illness and her death come installed in each of these new robots?

Even Dad wouldn't do that, would he?

"So what about you?" asked Leon. "What are your earliest memories?"

"I don't really need to tell you," I said. "They'll be exactly the same as yours."

He stood up and stepped closer. "So you've noticed it? How alike we are? It's so weird."

"You have no idea," I said.

He edged closer still. I could see a tiny bead of sweat running down his cheek. How had Dad even designed that? Fake sweat leaking from plastic pores?

Leon put his arms around me and pressed his lips to mine.

I really wanted to let it happen. I wanted to forget about the cruel experiment and pretend Leon was real. But I couldn't.

I backed away.

"I'm sorry," I said.

I ran back into the house.

CHAPTER 5

I tried to stay in my room and read the following day. A call from Dad flashed up on my phone after lunch, but I rejected it. I didn't feel like speaking to him.

I was sure he hadn't thought about the consequences when he was designing Leon. He'd programmed him with my tastes and my memories because I was the only teenager he knew.

That also made me the natural choice to test the robot out. But if he'd had any common sense at all, he'd have seen what would happen.

I'd meet a boy I felt totally suited to. We'd fall in love. And then I'd find out he wasn't real. What sort of a father would put his daughter through such torture?

It was difficult enough, even though I knew Leon was a robot.

I'd find myself putting my book down and staring at the wall. Leon's face would flash up and my heart would hammer. I'd tell it to stop and it would make no difference. It's like some animal part of my brain couldn't accept that he didn't really exist.

I tried to tell myself that having a crush on a robot was no worse than having a crush on a pop star. But it was. At least pop stars are human, even if the closest you're ever going to get to them is Row Z, Block 413. Falling in love with a machine is just wrong.

By mid-afternoon it was so hot I couldn't bear to stay in. But I didn't want to hang around the garden in case I saw Leon, so I decided to go out for a walk.

I strolled down the lane until I came to a gate with a footpath running beyond it. It led through a field where sheep were chewing on uneven grass. It looked like a perfect escape from the modern world of robots and computers.

I followed the path and saw a small hill beyond a clump of oak trees in the distance. It seemed like a good place to aim for.

I was just wondering if this was the hill the village was named after when I glanced over my shoulder and saw someone behind me.

Leon. He'd followed me from the house and now I couldn't avoid him. This was going to be awkward.

I waited for him to catch up. He was still wearing his gloves, as if he'd abandoned his work to follow me.

"I'm sorry about what happened yesterday," said Leon. "I shouldn't have tried it."

"It's fine," I said.

"I should have taken things more slowly," he said. "I hope I haven't ruined it."

He fixed his eyes on me and I looked away, scared to meet the gaze of a robot again. I was scared to speak, too, in case I hurt the feelings of a machine that couldn't possibly have any. I told myself to snap out of it.

"There's nothing to ruin," I said.

I could hear my voice wavering. My eyes were stinging too. Why was I working myself into a state over something that should have been as simple as shutting down a laptop?

"It could never work between us," I said.

Leon looked down at the ground and sighed.

"I understand," he said. "You're already with someone."

No, I thought. *I have no one and I want you. But you're nothing but a pile of plastic and circuits and second-hand memories. And even I'm not desperate enough to date that.*

"Yeah," I said. "Sorry."

Tears blurred my vision as I watched him walk away. I felt terrible, but it was nothing compared to what was to come.

CHAPTER 6

Dad came rushing up from his basement when I arrived home.

"Nice time in New York?" I asked.

"Didn't see much of the city," he said. It was scary how easily he slipped into his lie. "I spent the whole time in a lecture theatre. I hope your trip was more interesting."

I walked into the living room and plonked myself down on the couch. Dad followed me in.

"It was brilliant," I said. "Someone tried to fool me into making friends with a robot because they're a shameless liar. You'll be pleased to find out that I didn't fall for it."

Dad slumped down in an armchair and let out a deep breath. "Oh dear," he said. "I really thought I was onto something with the M35–50. What gave it away?"

"No!" I yelled. "We're not going to sit here and discuss your stupid machine. We're going to talk about the trick you played on me. Have you any idea how it made me feel?"

"The test had to be secret, dear," he said. "They always are."

I folded my arms and waited for an apology. It didn't come.

I might have told him how I'd really known Leon was a robot if he'd said sorry. But he didn't so I let him suffer.

I went up to my room and I listened to Dad pacing around downstairs. He obviously wasn't sure how long he should leave me.

In the end, he held out for twenty minutes.

"I'm sorry the test upset you so much," he said from the other side of my door. "I had no idea it would."

"Well it did," I said.

"If you're ready to tell me how you worked it out it would be really useful," he said. "We can do it in my workshop if you like. I've got a few other M35–50 models down there. They might help you to remember what you noticed."

I felt my heart racing. There were other Leons just two floors beneath me. I could be reunited with him in just a few seconds.

And then what? Form a stupid crush on a robot again and go back to beating myself up?

On the other hand, maybe seeing a row of Leons lined up in the workshop would finally stop me obsessing over him. It. Them. Whatever.

I followed Dad down to the basement. I felt like my legs were about to give way as I made my way down the creaky stairs.

Dad unlocked the door and swung it open. He walked inside, fumbled along the wall and flipped a switch.

Bright strip lights flicked on to reveal his messy workshop with its jumble of circuit boards and metal limbs.

I looked at the far wall and gasped. Four identical robots were lined up against it. They turned to me and smiled.

They all looked exactly like my uncle.

CHAPTER 7

"Where's Leon?" I asked. "The robot who was doing the gardening? About my age, tall, good looking."

"I don't know who you mean," said Dad. He pointed at the line of uncle robots and they stared at his finger. "This was the robot I sent you to test. The M35–50. It stands for 'male between 35 and 50'."

"Don't tell me Leon was human," I said. I felt my heart plunge. "He can't have been."

Dad was overjoyed, of course. Not only had his machine fooled me, it had done so when I'd been on the lookout for a robot. It had passed the test as well as it could have done.

Dad designed his robot to be as unremarkable as possible. He wanted someone who'd fade into the background and that's what he got. I never questioned whether the uncle I hadn't seen for years was the robot, and I'm sure millions of others will be fooled into thinking it's human too.

Dad thinks the M35–50 is going to make us rich, and he could be right. But I'm not thinking about that right now. I'm thinking about Leon.

I met someone I could talk to without feeling embarrassed, someone who liked the same stuff as me, someone who saw the world the way I do.

And how did I treat him? I ignored him, I pushed him away, I rejected him, I pretended I already had a boyfriend.

I met my Mr Perfect. And I really messed up.

THE END